STARTING OUT

baby
TIGERS

KATE RIGGS

CREATIVE EDUCATION • CREATIVE PAPERBACKS

CONT

ENTS

I AM A CUB.

I am a baby tiger.

ear

nose

paw

I weighed **about two** pounds (0.9 kg) at birth. My eyes stayed closed for two weeks.

Our <u>litter</u> **stays** in the **den** for eight weeks. Soon we will use our sharp teeth to eat meat.

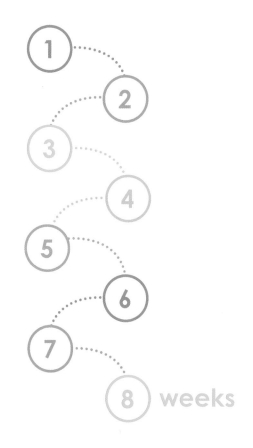

1
2
3
4
5
6
7
8 weeks

Hunting is hard! It takes more than a year for me to learn.

I track down my own meals.

I am a young tiger now!

SPEAK AND LISTEN

GRRRRRA

AARRR.!

Can you speak like a cub?

Tigers yip, growl, and roar.

Listen to these sounds:

https://www.youtube.com
/watch?v=cNx0E-SXTAY

Now it is
your turn!

CUB WORDS

den: a small, hidden area where an animal rests

fur: the hair that covers some animals

litter: the group of animals born at one time

READING CORNER

Hall, Margaret. *Tigers and Their Cubs*. North Mankato, Minn.: Capstone Press, 2018.

Meister, Cari. *Do You Really Want to Meet a Tiger?* North Mankato, Minn.: Amicus, 2015.

Nilsen, Genevieve. *Tiger Cubs*. Minneapolis: Jump!, 2019.

INDEX

PUBLISHED BY CREATIVE EDUCATION AND CREATIVE PAPERBACKS
P.O. Box 227, Mankato, Minnesota 56002
Creative Education and Creative Paperbacks
are imprints of The Creative Company
www.thecreativecompany.us

LIBRARY OF CONGRESS CATALOGING-IN-PUBLICATION DATA
Names: Riggs, Kate, author.
Title: Baby tigers / Kate Riggs.
Series: Starting out.
Summary: A baby tiger narrates the story of its life, describing how physical features, diet, habitat, and familial relationships play a role in its growth and development.

Identifiers: ISBN 978-1-64026-252-2 (hardcover)
ISBN 978-1-62832-815-8 (pbk)
ISBN 978-1-64000-393-4 (eBook)
This title has been submitted for CIP processing
under LCCN 2019938712.

CCSS: RI.K.1, 2, 3, 4, 5, 6, 7; RI.1.1, 2, 3, 4, 5, 6, 7;
RF.K.1, 3; RF.1.1

DESIGN AND PRODUCTION
by Chelsey Luther and Joe Kahnke
Art direction by Rita Marshall
Printed in the United States of America

PHOTOGRAPHS by Getty Images (Martin Harvey/DigitalVision), iStockphoto (GlobalP), Minden Pictures (Suzi Eszterhas, Andy Rouse/NPL), Shutterstock (Bohbeh, cosma, Eric Isselee, Anan Kaewkhammul, Dagmara Ksandrova, Ultrashock)

FIRST EDITION HC 9 8 7 6 5 4 3 2 1
FIRST EDITION PBK 9 8 7 6 5 4 3 2 1